THIS WALKER BOOK BELONGS TO:

_____

_____

_____

_____

For ABC and all his
grandchildren
  T.C.

For Roslyn and Phillip
  S.W.

First published 2000 by Walker Books Ltd
87 Vauxhall Walk, London SE11 5HJ

This edition published 2001

10 9 8 7 6 5 4 3 2 1

Text © 2000 Trish Cooke
Illustrations © 2000 Sharon Wilson

This book has been typeset in Leawood Book

Printed in Hong Kong

British Library Cataloguing in Publication Data:
a catalogue record for this book is available
from the British Library

ISBN 0-7445-7875-2

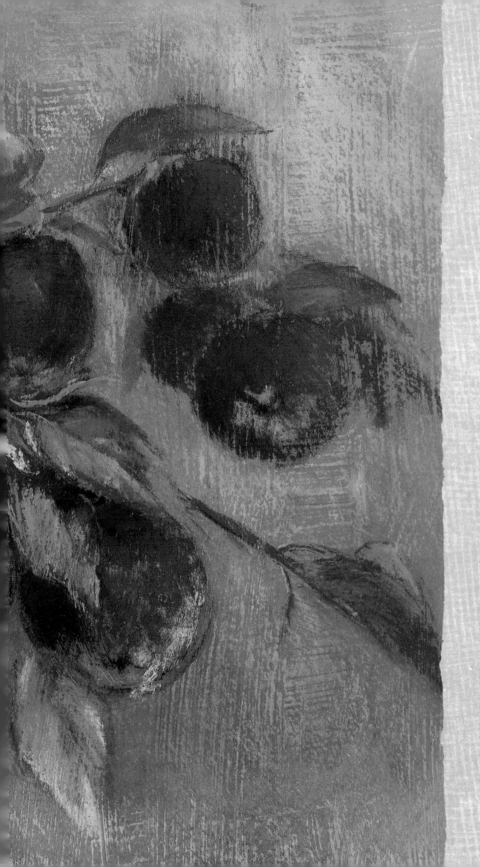

THE GRANDAD TREE

Trish Cooke

illustrated by
Sharon Wilson

WALKER BOOKS
AND SUBSIDIARIES
LONDON · BOSTON · SYDNEY

There is a tree
at the bottom of Leigh's garden.
An apple tree.
Vin, Leigh's big brother, said
it started as a seed
and then grew
and grew.
And Vin said
that tree,
where they used to play
with Grandad,
that apple tree
will be there ...
for ever.

Their grandad
was a baby once
and he grew
and grew.
Vin said
Grandad went to school
and he climbed
coconut trees,
and looked out at the sea
from the top.

And when he was a man
he was a husband for their gran
and a dad
for their mam
   and Auntie Melissa
      and Uncle Victor
and then
a grandad for them.

"That's life,"
their grandad used to say.

In the spring
the apple tree
is covered in white blossom.

In the summer
the apples grow.

In the autumn
the leaves fall off.

In the winter
it is covered in snow.

And sometimes things die,
like trees,
like people ...
    like Grandad.

But they don't go away
for ever.
They stay ...
because
we remember.

Leigh planted a seed
for Grandad,
just beside the apple tree.
And when she is sad
Vin takes her hand,
and he waters the seed
with Leigh.

And it will grow and grow,
and it will go
through changes

and they'll love it
    for ever and ever ...

just like they'll always

love Grandad.

TRISH COOKE wrote *The Grandad Tree* after watching her son's reaction to the death of her father. "Kieron, then aged four, was very curious, and started burying dead insects in the garden," she says. "As I watched him doing this one day, under the apple tree, it came to me that everything has its natural cycle, and the changes in the apple tree through the seasons seemed to express this simply and clearly."

Trish Cooke is a well-known presenter on the BBC children's television programme, *Playdays* and has written and acted in plays for television and theatre. Her books for Walker include *So Much*, winner of the 1994 Kurt Maschler Award, the 0–5 category of the Smarties Book Prize and Highly Commended for the 1995 Kate Greenaway Medal; *When I Grow Bigger* and *Mr Pam Pam and the Hullabazoo*. Trish lives in Bradford with her partner and their two children.

SHARON WILSON says, "I wanted to illustrate *The Grandad Tree* from the first moment I read the manuscript. The memories of my grandad are so strong and wonderful, I wanted to share those feelings with others."

Sharon Wilson trained at the Massachusetts College of Art in Boston, USA. Since then she has illustrated two other picture books, *The Day Gogo Went to Vote: South Africa, 1994* and *Freedom's Gifts: A Juneteenth Story*. Sharon lives in Bermuda.

ISBN 0-7445-4396-7 (pb)

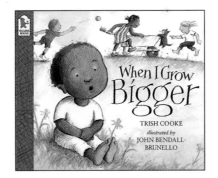

ISBN 0-7445-4327-4 (pb)

ISBN 0-7445-4311-8 (pb)